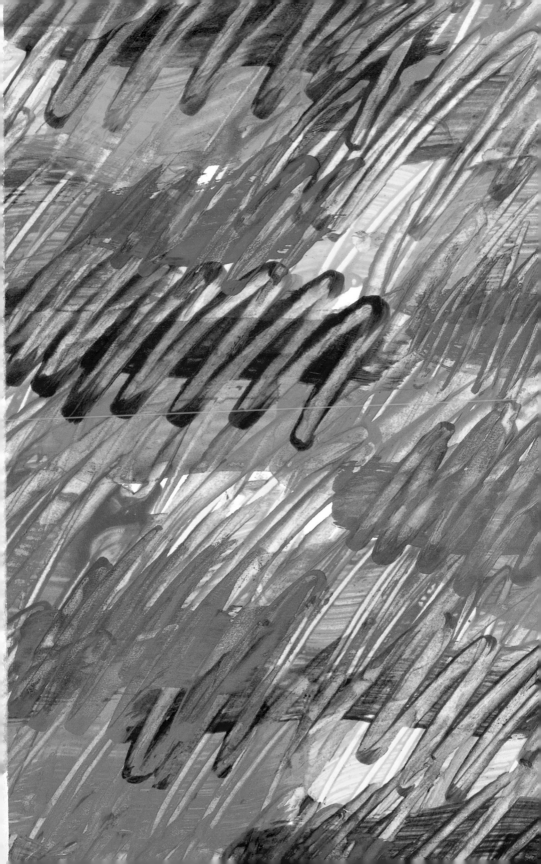

For Sally and Bob

Dear Parents and Educators,

Welcome to Penguin Young Readers! As parents and educators, you know that each child develops at his or her own pace—in terms of speech, critical thinking, and, of course, reading. Penguin Young Readers recognizes this fact. As a result, each Penguin Young Readers book is assigned a traditional easy-to-read level (1–4) as well as a Guided Reading Level (A–P). Both of these systems will help you choose the right book for your child. Please refer to the back of each book for specific leveling information. Penguin Young Readers features esteemed authors and illustrators, stories about favorite characters, fascinating nonfiction, and more!

The Very Quiet Cricket

LEVEL **3**

GUIDED
READING
LEVEL **K**

This book is perfect for a **Transitional Reader** who:
- can read multisyllable and compound words;
- can read words with prefixes and suffixes;
- is able to identify story elements (beginning, middle, end, plot, setting, characters, problem, solution); and
- can understand different points of view.

Here are some **activities** you can do during and after reading this book:
- List all the words in the story that have an -ed ending. On a separate sheet of paper, write the root word next to the word with the -ed ending, using the chart below as an example.

word with an -ed ending	root word
chirped	chirp
rubbed	rub
wanted	want

- Setting: The setting of the story is where it takes place. Discuss the setting or settings of this story. Use some evidence from the text to describe the setting.

Remember, sharing the love of reading with a child is the best gift you can give!

—Bonnie Bader, EdM
  Penguin Young Readers program

*Penguin Young Readers are leveled by independent reviewers applying the standards developed by Irene Fountas and Gay Su Pinnell in *Matching Books to Readers: Using Leveled Books in Guided Reading*, Heinemann, 1999.

PENGUIN YOUNG READERS
Published by the Penguin Group
Penguin Group (USA) LLC, 375 Hudson Street, New York, New York 10014, USA

USA | Canada | UK | Ireland | Australia | New Zealand | India | South Africa | China

penguin.com
A Penguin Random House Company

The Library of Congress has cataloged the Philomel edition under the following Control Number: 8978317

ISBN 978-0-448-48138-8 (pbk)   10 9 8 7 6 5 4 3 2 1
ISBN 978-0-448-48139-5 (hc)   10 9 8 7 6 5 4 3 2

The Very
Quiet Cricket

by Eric Carle

Penguin Young Readers
An Imprint of Penguin Group (USA) LLC

One warm day, from a tiny egg
a little cricket was born.

Welcome! chirped a big cricket,

rubbing his wings together.

The little cricket wanted to answer,

so he rubbed his wings together.

But nothing happened.

Not a sound.

Good morning! whizzed a locust,

spinning through the air.

The little cricket wanted

to answer, so he rubbed

his wings together.

But nothing happened.

Not a sound.

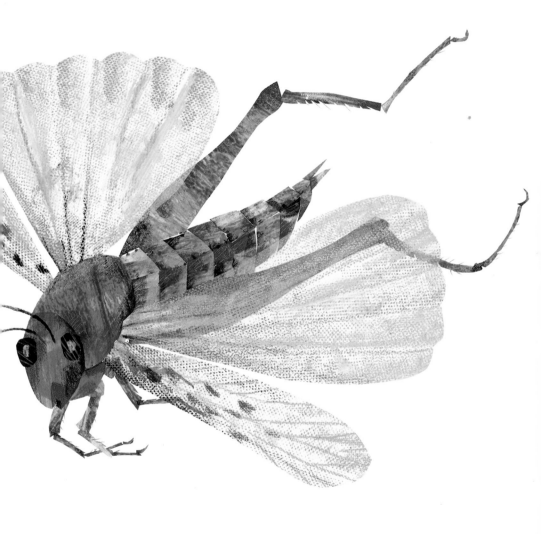

Hello! whispered a praying mantis, scraping its huge front legs together.

The little cricket wanted
to answer, so he rubbed
his wings together.
But nothing happened.
Not a sound.

Good day! crunched a worm,
munching its way out of
an apple.

12

The little cricket wanted to
answer, so he rubbed
his wings together.
But nothing happened.
Not a sound.

Hi! bubbled a spittlebug,

slurping in a sea of froth.

The little cricket wanted to

answer, so he rubbed

his wings together.

But nothing happened.

Not a sound.

Good afternoon!
screeched a cicada,
clinging to a branch
of a tree.
The little cricket
wanted to answer,
so he rubbed his
wings together.

But nothing happened.

Not a sound.

How are you! hummed

a bumblebee, flying from

flower to flower.

The little cricket wanted

to answer, so he rubbed his

wings together.

But nothing happened.

Not a sound.

Good evening! whirred

a dragonfly, gliding above

the water.

The little cricket wanted to answer,
so he rubbed his wings together.
But nothing happened.
Not a sound.

Good night! buzzed the
mosquitoes, dancing among
the stars.

little cricket wanted to answer,

so he rubbed his wings together.

But nothing happened.

Not a sound.

A luna moth sailed quietly

through the night.

And the cricket enjoyed

the stillness.

And this time he chirped the
most beautiful sound that she
had ever heard.

There are 4,000 different kinds of crickets. Some live underground, others above. Some live in shrubs or trees, and some even live in water.

Both male and female crickets can hear, but only the male can make a sound.

By rubbing his wings together he chirps. Some people say that it sounds like a song!